For HuDson Leigh,
The Biggest Blether I know

written By
Gerry Cav

illustrations By
Brenda Bossato

INSTAGRAM-StoriesByGerryCav FACEBOOK-StoriesByGerryCav

# Oban's Own Dinosaur

## (Forget Nessie)

PUBLISHED IN 2019 THROUGH A PARTNERSHIP

WITH Partick Whistle Ltd

Text & Story©Gerry Cav

Illustrations©Brenda Bossato (Instagram@brendabossatoart)

INSTAGRAM/StoriesByGerryCav

FACEBOOK/StoriesByGerryCav

Many people of the small coastal town of Oban have heard the rumours of a dinosaur living there,

and a few claim to have seen it.

If you look hard enough at McCaig's Tower at night, high above Oban,

you might just see a shadow that resembles the shape of a dinosaur.

Every morning at dawn, a seagull named Gully, will fly up to the tower to awaken his dinosaur friend.

Then again at dusk, just to say goodnight to his pal.

You may have already asked yourself, how does a dinosaur end up living in Oban? Well, one night, a heavy sea storm changed this quiet fishing town, when a large egg was swept onto the Oban shores.

When that egg hatched on that wet and windy night, a baby Brachiosaurus found itself wet, afraid and all alone.

The spotlights shinning bright from McCaig's Tower caught the dinosaur's eye.

With nowhere else to go, it decided to climb up the steep hill, towards the tower.

Inside McCaig's Tower, the dinosaur found protection under a tree, behind the large sturdy granite walls.

With nowhere else to go, it curled up into a ball and closed its eyes.

The very next morning, Gully and the dinosaur met for the very first time.
"What is your name little dinosaur?" the seagull asked.
"I don't have a name yet," replied the dinosaur.
"You have a very long neck, little dinosaur, how about we call you Neckie. Hiya Neckie, my name is Gully the Seagull," Gully said with excitement.

Eventually, Neckie got used to life in Oban. During the day, he would go looking for food, which soon helped Neckie grow into a big and strong Brachiosaurus.

"Gully, it gets harder for me to find enough food to fill my belly. I eat and I eat, but I just get hungry again," Neckie said, worryingly.

"If you want, Neckie, you can have some of my fresh worms? They're my favourite," said Gully.

"Worms? Yuck, no thanks, you save those worms for a non-rainy day pal," Neckie said, with disgust.

One night at dusk, Gully flew up to the tower to see his pal. But Neckie was nowhere to be seen.

Gully is always worried about Neckie, and so he imagines the worst.

If caught, could Neckie end up inside a huge cage at the zoo?

Where people would point at Neckie and take pictures of him all day long?

When Gully couldn't
find Neckie anywhere,
he panicked. He knew
he had to find him,
and fast!

Gully flew high above Oban, in search of Neckie, until he came across a deer. Gully decided to land in order to question the deer.

"Hiya pal, have you seen a dinosaur with a long neck around here?" asked Gully.

"Oh you mean Neckie? He was here this morning," the deer replied.

Earlier that day, Neckie and the deer had shared a moment together:

"Apple?" Neckie asked the deer.

"Yes please, my first ever apple.

I have never been tall enough to get one for myself," replied the deer.

"Whoah, it's soooo juicy!" the deer added, after taking a bite.

"If you wait until autumn, the apples will fall to the ground all by themselves. Especially the juicy ones," explained Gully.
"Oh yum," replied the deer.

The deer then pointed in the direction of where Neckie went next.

Gully was on the move again, until he came across a Highland Cow.

"Hiya pal, have you seen a dinosaur with a very long neck around here?" asked Gully.

The Highland Cow then told Gully of his encounter with Neckie earlier that day.

"Hey Neckie, are you eating with us today?" asked the Highland Cow. "Do you have anything a bit sweeter than regular old grass?" asked Neckie.

"Well there is some rhubarb in the bushes," the Highland Cow suggested.

"Rhubarb is such a funny word, don't you think? Even saying it with a mouthful of rhubarb, you can still hear that I'm actually saying rhubarb. That makes me giggle," Neckie says, while laughing to himself.

"Once Neckie ate some rhubarb, he went down towards the beach," the Highland Cow told Gully.

When Gully got to the beach, there was only a Puffin, and no sign of Neckie.

"Hiya pal, has a dinosaur with a very long neck come by here?" Gully asked.

"Yeah, you just missed Neckie. He was wandering around the beach looking for food," said the Puffin.

The Puffin then told Gully, how he met Neckie that day.
"This is my spot," said the Puffin in an angry voice.
"What is your spot?" asked Neckie.

"My spot to catch fish," explained the Puffin.
"But I don't eat fish, I'm a herbivore," replied Neckie.
"What is a herbivore?" asked the confused Puffin.

"I can't physically eat meat; my teeth are too small and so I can only chew vegetables," explained Neckie.

"Oh really, follow me! I know where some seaweed is, that you can eat," said the Puffin, eagerly.

"After he ate, Neckie went south along the beach," said the Puffin.

Once again, Gully flew off into the sky.

At long last, Gully found his pal, but strangely, Neckie was running along the beach with hay in his mouth.

"Neckie... Neckie!" Gully shouted from the sky.

"I've been all over Oban looking for you!" states Gully.

"I'm so sorry, Gully, I just couldn't leave it on it's own," said Neckie, sounding scared.

"Leave what on its own?" a confused Gully asked.

"Neckie, is that a dinosaur egg?" Gully asked, with shear shock. "Quick Gully, we need more hay to cover it, to keep it warm," shouts a frightened Neckie.

Neckie then turns around and starts rushing away, to get more hay.

"It's too late, the egg is already hatching," declared Gully.

The egg slowly hatches, and out pops a baby triceratops

The baby dinosaur slowly crawls out of the egg, only to be distracted by the sound of the waves.

Before Gully and Neckie could react, the baby dinosaur is running along the shore of the sea, before splashing into the water.

"Gully, please can we call him splash?" laughs Neckie.

"Splash, the baby dinosaur, it is!" Gully replied, laughing.

Neckie and Gully take Splash up the hill with them, to McCaig's Tower. Both dinosaurs fall asleep together, under the watchful eye of Gully and the twinkling stars above.

And that, my fruity friends is the story of how Oban became the home of two resident dinosaurs.

But wheesht, don't tell anyone, as it's Oban's longest kept secret!

If you ever stop by Oban, why not leave some vegetables at McCaig's Tower for our dinosaur pals?

And you might just get a cheeky wink,

from a certain friendly seagull.

# Theeeeeeeeee End

Made in the USA
Middletown, DE
04 October 2020